Outbreak

Outbreak

Alison Prince

Illustrated by Grahame Baker Smith

A & C BLACK
AN IMPRINT OF BLOOMSBURY
LONDON NEW DELHI NEW YORK SYDNEY

White Wolves Series Consultant: Sue Ellis,
Centre for Literacy in Primary Education

This book can be used in the White Wolves Guided Reading
programme with more experienced readers at Year 4 level

First published 2008 by A & C Black,
an imprint of Bloomsbury Publishing Plc
50 Bedford Square, London, WC1B 3DP

www.bloomsbury.com

Text copyright © 2008 Alison Prince
Illustrations copyright © 2008 Grahame Baker Smith

The rights of Alison Prince and Grahame Baker Smith to
be identified as author and illustrator of this work respectively
have been asserted by them in accordance with the
Copyrights, Designs and Patents Act 1988.

ISBN 978-0-7136-8840-5

A CIP catalogue for this book is available from the British Library.

This book is produced using paper that is made from wood grown in
managed, sustainable forests. It is natural, renewable and recyclable.
The logging and manufacturing processes conform to the
environmental regulations of the country of origin.

Printed and bound in Great Britain
by CPI Group (UK), Croydon, CR0 4YY

5 7 9 10 8 6

Contents

Contents

Chapter One
Puzzle

I don't know what Mum is up to. Every week, she buys a bit more stuff than we need. Sugar, tinned fruit and baked beans, sardines, tea and coffee, bars of chocolate.

She stacks it in the high cupboard in the kitchen, which we never usually use.

Why do we need such a lot?

This morning, Mum was looking at a photo in the newspaper. "Poor souls," she said.

She wasn't really talking to me, but I went to see what she was looking at.

The photo showed a muddy road with people walking along it. They were carrying heavy suitcases and bundles. A couple of families had piled all their things on carts pulled by horses.

"Some people called Nazis have come to power in Germany," Mum told me. "They are doing terrible things, and these families have to leave their homes."

"But why?" I asked.

"The Nazis say Germany should only be for people who are pure Germans. Anyone else will be sent to a prison camp."

She seemed really upset.

"What do you mean, 'pure'?"

"Someone who has parents and grandparents who are German," she explained. "Not mixed with people from any other country. Especially not Jews."

"Where are the people going?" I asked.

"They're hoping to get to France," Mum said. "The French are like us – they don't like the Nazis, either." Then she folded the paper and said, "Don't you worry about it. Go and play in the garden. It's a lovely day."

There's a swing in the garden, among the cherry trees, so I went out there like Mum said, and swung for a bit, but I kept thinking about the people with their cases and bundles. I'd hate to leave this house, and the cherry trees, and Smudge. He's my cat, and he's beautiful.

When Dad came in from work
this evening, he said, "Hello,
sweetheart. How's my Mandy?"

I thought he meant someone
else, but he was smiling at me.
I frowned and said, "I'm Miriam."

"Mandy is a nickname," said
Mum.

I frowned again and said,
"I don't want a nickname."

"We think it's really nice,"
said Mum.

After I went to bed, I could
hear Dad playing the piano
downstairs, same as he always
does, but things seemed kind
of different.

Pam is older than me, but she's
my best friend. She lives just up
the road. We were upstairs in her
bedroom today, and I told her
about Dad calling me Mandy. She
nodded, as if she knew all about it.

"It's because Miriam is a Jewish name," she said. "Your mother was here the other day, talking to my mum, and she mentioned it. They didn't think I could hear, but I was in the dining room and they were in the kitchen, and you can hear through the serving hatch."

I get a bit fed up with Pam knowing everything. I know things, too. "There are Nazis in Germany," I told her. "People are leaving their homes, in case they get sent to prison camps."

But Pam knew about that, too. "Yes," she agreed. "And the Nazis invaded Czechoslovakia a couple of months ago. Your mum thinks Britain should have declared war on them because of that, but a lot of people think it's nothing to do with us. If the Nazis come here, though, it might be dangerous for you to have a Jewish name."

I was a bit scared. "Do you think they will come?" I asked.

Pam shrugged. "Don't know."

Then her mum shouted up the stairs for Pam to hurry, because they were getting the bus to the library, so we didn't say any more.

Mum put two more bags of sugar in the high cupboard this morning.

I said, "Are you saving things up because there's going to be a war?"

She got down off the chair she was standing on, and put it back at the table. Then she said, "Who told you there's going to be a war?"

"Pam did," I said.

Mum sighed. "Well, yes, there may be," she said. "And if there is, food will be short. Britain gets a lot of things from overseas, and our ships will be under attack."

Then she ruffled my hair and said, "Don't look so worried. It may not happen. And we're going on holiday next week. That'll be nice, won't it!"

We're going to the seaside. I wish we could take Smudge, but it's a long way on the train and Dad said, "Don't be silly, love, he'd hate it." Pam says she will come in every day and feed him.

Chapter Two
Seaside

We can't go on the beach. There are rolls of barbed wire all over it, and big, metal spikes sticking out of the sand, pointing towards the sea.

Dad says the spikes are to stop tanks. I've seen pictures of tanks. They have a big gun at the front, and they run on caterpillars.

There are enormous guns all the way along the cliffs, with long barrels that reach into the sky above our heads.

I put my hands over my ears every time we go past them, because I'm scared that one might go off. I hate loud bangs.

Dad said, "They won't go off. They're only there in case the Germans come."

But our soldiers might want to fire them just for practice, so I still put my hands over my ears.

Mrs Bingley, who owns our boarding house, always calls me Mandy. I suppose it's what Mum and Dad told her. She argues with Mum about the war. She says

Mr Chamberlain, our Prime Minister, won't let it happen. He came back from a meeting in Germany last year saying there will be 'peace for our time'.

Mum said, "He gave the Nazis part of Czechoslovakia. But they won't be satisfied with that."

It's not much fun here, really. We go for walks and sit in cafés, but I want to paddle in the sea and make sand castles, and you can't go on the beach anywhere.

We went to the funfair yesterday, and I won a teapot shaped like a cottage, but it doesn't pour very well. We're going home tomorrow. It'll be nice to see Smudge.

Church bells are not to be rung any more. If we hear them, it will mean the German troops have invaded. I thought of the spikes on the beach, and the rolls of barbed wire. Maybe the invaders' warships will blow all that stuff up, and their tanks will roll in across our fields and along our roads. It's very scary.

This morning, Mum and Dad told me we're going to stay with Gran in the country.

I asked, "For another holiday?" and they looked at each other.

Then Dad said, "No, it's longer than a holiday. We'll be there for a while."

"But what about school?" I said. "Term starts next week."

"I'll help you with some lessons," said Mum. "Gran's got lots of books. We can do nature study. There's lots of nature in the country."

There's a big pine forest next

to Gran's house. It's very dark
and quiet, and you can get lost
in it easily, because it all looks the
same. Gran always has her back
door open for the birds. She's mad
about birds. She puts chopped-up
cheese on the table so the robin
can help himself.

"I suppose we can't take
Smudge," I said.

"I'm sorry, darling," said Mum.
"But you know how Gran feels
about her birds."

"Can't I stay here?" I asked.
"I can cook and everything.
Smudge and I would be all right."

"No, sweetheart, you can't,"
said Dad. He gave me a hug and
added, "What would we
do without you?"

Pam's dad drove us in his car, because we were taking so much stuff. His name is Bob. Mum brought quite a lot of things from the high cupboard in the kitchen, so she must think we're going for ages.

Bob said that petrol will be rationed when the war starts. He's a salesman, so he thinks he'll be able to keep his car, but he says most people won't be allowed to drive at all.

Mum and I sat in the back. She was leaning forward so she could hear what Bob and Dad were saying, but I felt a bit carsick, so I had my eyes shut. I think they thought I was asleep, but I wasn't.

"It'll be an early start for you in the mornings, getting to work in London," Bob said to my dad. "You're a long way from the city."

Dad said, "I know that. But I can't take the risk."

"Look on the bright side," Bob said. "They may not invade."

"But they might," said Dad. "So it's better to be out of London. Just going to the bank every day should be all right. If they pick me up, I'll be interned – but at least my family will be safe."

I wanted to know what 'interned' meant, so I opened my eyes and sat up, but Mum said quickly, "Hello, darling – are you feeling better? Let's play 'I Spy'." So I never got the chance to ask.

Chapter Three
At Gran's

It's very quiet here. The days are warm and sleepy. Blue Michaelmas daisies bloom in Gran's untidy garden, and the sky is almost the same deep colour, without a cloud.

There are boxes of apples and plums outside every cottage gate for people to help themselves. The bruised fruits turn brown and smell rotten and spicy, and wasps buzz over them.

Gran has plenty of apples from the trees in her garden, so we don't need to dip into the boxes. I'm glad – I'd hate to be stung. I'm quite a coward, really.

This morning they tested the air-raid siren, and we nearly jumped out of our skins. The siren is on the roof of the police station in the village, and it's really loud.

It started with a wail that went up and up then down again, and kept going up and down for about two minutes, until it tailed away. That will be the warning signal, to tell us that enemy aircraft are coming.

When they've gone, the siren will sound the All Clear, which means it rises to a steady note and stays on it.

I don't have much to do, really.
Mum seems to have forgotten
about lessons. She and Gran are
busy using up the apples. They
bottle them, and make jelly and
chutney.

Today they were in the front room, making blackout curtains. Everyone has to make sure there's no light showing in their windows, in case enemy aircraft see it and drop bombs on us.

I was in the kitchen, listening to the radio.
A woman who had escaped from Germany was talking.

She said children over there had sometimes accidentally betrayed their parents to the Nazis. They didn't mean to – they'd perhaps just said something at school or to a friend that made it clear they were Jewish. Then armed men came banging at the door in the middle of the night and took the whole family away, and they were never seen again. The woman said they were interned in prison camps, and a lot of them were being killed.

I keep thinking about what Dad said to Bob in the car: *If they pick me up, I'll be interned.* It means, if the Nazis find him, they will put him in a prison camp. Perhaps he and Mum have been afraid of that for a long time, so they have never told me about being Jewish, in case I accidentally betray them. But I never would. Couldn't they have trusted me? I'd rather die that let anything bad happen to them. I am ashamed now that I made a fuss about being called Mandy.

I mustn't tell Mum and Dad I've guessed their secret, or they'll worry. I will keep it faithfully. Nobody will ever get it out of me.

We had to go to the village hall today, to get our gas masks. They are made of black rubber, with a transparent bit in front of your eyes so you can see out.

You put the mask on by pushing your chin into it first, then pulling the webbing straps over your head.

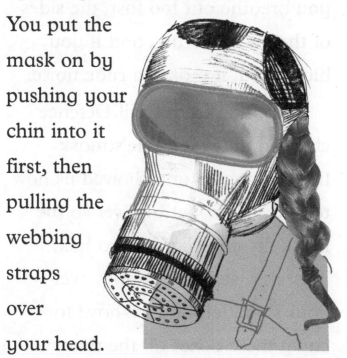

The rubbery smell is horrible. The air comes in through a round metal bit that has a filter inside to stop poison gas coming in. When you breathe out, you can feel warm air going past your ears. If you breathe out too fast, the sides of the mask vibrate, and if you blow hard, it makes a rude noise.

The man from Civil Defence checked that everyone's mask fitted properly, and showed us how to fold the rubber bit over so the mask fits in its cardboard box. There's a string that goes over your shoulder, and we have to carry these boxes all the time.

The village hall stayed open late, and Dad went down to get his mask when he came home from his work in London. There are no gas masks for cats. I'm praying we don't have a gas attack.

Chapter Four
War

Today is September 1st. The Nazis have invaded Poland.

Mum said, "Now we *must* go to war."

She and Gran started talking about how the Germans have thousands of tanks and the Poles have only a hundred or so. They said Mr Chamberlain has told the Nazis they must get out of Poland, but they are taking no notice.

40

I went into the kitchen. The robin flew up from the table, and out of the door. I wish I could fly away like that.

This morning, the war began. It's a Sunday, so Dad was at home. September 3rd, 1939. It's a date I will always remember. I was outside Gran's house, drawing a pattern in the sandy lane with a stick – when Mum rushed out and grabbed me.

"Come in, quickly!" she said.

I thought I'd done something wrong at first, but she wasn't cross, just agitated. She bundled me into the kitchen, where the radio was on. A serious voice was talking. Our four gas masks were standing on the dresser. Gran had taken them out of their boxes, ready for use, and she was sprinkling talcum powder into them.

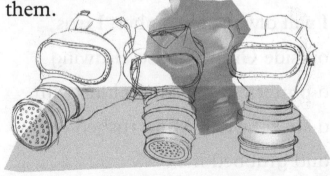

"It'll make them smell nicer if we have to wear them," she said.

I thought the powder might make me sneeze. I started to ask what would happen if you sneezed in a mask – but Mum hushed me.

Mr Chamberlain, the Prime Minister, had started to speak. He said, "This morning the British Ambassador in Berlin handed the German Government a final note, stating that unless we heard from them by 11.00 a.m. that they were prepared at once to withdraw their troops from Poland, a state of war would exist between us."

Gran put her hand to her mouth, but none of us said anything.

The voice on the radio went on.

"I have to tell you that no such undertaking has been received, and that consequently this country is at war with Germany."

"Oh, dear God," breathed Mum.

She and Dad and Gran stared at each other.

Mr Chamberlain was still speaking. I didn't understand most of it, but some words made sense. "He can only be stopped by force … we and France … going to the aid of Poland … I know that you will play your part with calmness and courage."

We listened to the end. And at that moment, as if to make this war come absolutely true, the air-raid siren sounded. Its rising-and-falling wail was far louder than the radio, and Mum put her arm round me and pulled me close.

We listened for the hum of aircraft engines, for gunfire and explosions, but there was nothing. Dad switched the radio off, and there was silence.

After a few minutes, the All Clear sounded. When it died away, there were footsteps outside, and Gran's next-door neighbour put her head round the kitchen door.

"Do you think it's safe to go out in the garden?" she said. "I've ever such a lot of peas waiting to be picked."

We all laughed.

Gran had started putting the gas masks back in their boxes. "Hitler can't stop us picking peas," she said.

Chapter Five
Not Well

I'm kind of shaky, and I feel cold
even though the autumn sun goes
on shining. I miss Smudge. I want
to cry every time I think about
him. It's hard to eat anything –
it just seems too difficult.

At night, I'm scared to go to sleep because of awful dreams. Mum says she thinks I haven't enough to do. She told me to listen to Schools Broadcasts on the radio, but I listen to other things as well.

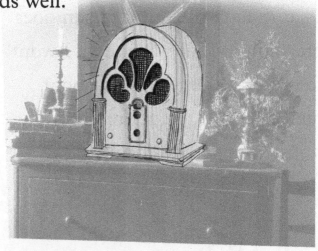

A few days ago I heard someone talking about a man who was captured by the Nazis.

They tortured him to try and make him tell them what he knew. They pulled out his fingernails, and then they beat him until he died, but he still did not tell.

In my dreams I'm never brave enough. I can't stop the soldiers from taking Mum and Dad away.

I am in a room with men who are going to torture me. They have strapped me in a chair so I can't move. I feel sick and shivery.

Mum took my temperature this afternoon, and put me to bed.

The doctor came today. He felt my pulse and asked me to stick out my tongue and listened to my chest, then he sat and looked at me.

"I think you may be worried," he said. He had a kind voice that sounded a bit foreign.

I shook my head, but tears started to come. I couldn't stop them.

He said, "Tell me?"

It was hard to speak. After a minute, I said, "I am not brave."

"Neither am I," the doctor said. He handed me a hanky and I blew my nose. He asked, "Why do you have to be brave?"

It sounded silly, when I started to tell him. The Nazis are not here yet. Perhaps they never will be. But he listened, and did not smile.

Mum was really upset. She took my hand and said, "Darling, we only wanted to keep you safe."

"But... I didn't know," I said, and started to cry again because not knowing seemed to be the thing that hurt. "You didn't tell me."

And then it all came tumbling out. I told them about the story I'd heard on the radio, and the terrible dreams.

"I think you are brave, Miriam," the doctor said. "It's hard to tell anyone about secret things that hurt you." Then he went on, "I am from Poland – the country the Nazis have just invaded. But I left there three years ago, before they came.

"I ran away to England with my wife. My mother and father said they were too old to start a new life in another country, so they stayed behind. I don't know what will happen to them now. We are Jews, you see."

He and my mother looked at

each other, then Mum said quietly,
"What can we do?"

"I think you should go home,"
the doctor said. "Running away
does not stop you from being
afraid. Unknown dangers are
much more frightening than
known ones."

All that was last year. We came home, and I went back to school. Smudge was all right, though he was very glad to see us.

The Nazis did not invade. Mum says they have too much on their hands in Europe to think of coming here – but she thinks this war is going to be a long one.

We have an air-raid shelter in the garden, under the cherry tree. It's summer now, and the war is happening in the sky.

We watch the patterns of white vapour trails and hear the rattle of machine guns as the small aeroplanes wheel and dive.

Sometimes one of them is hit and goes spinning down, trailing smoke and flame. I hate to think of the men inside it.

But I am not afraid.

About the Author

Alison has written about 45 books for children, but says she's lost count. She won the Guardian Children's Fiction Award for *The Sherwood Hero* and has several times won the Scottish Arts Council's Children's Book of the Year prize. She grew up during World War II, and *Outbreak* has a lot to do with her own memories of that time – especially Miriam's worry about her cat!

Other White Wolves
historical stories...

THE
QUEEN'S
TOKEN

Pamela Oldfield

Hal is a poor stable boy, who has a
dream – to work for King Henry at
his palace in Whitehall. But when
he chances upon the royal party, it's
not the meeting he'd hoped for. He's
accused of being a spy and his fate
now rests in the king's hands... Will
Henry live up to his fierce reputation,
or will Hal live another day?

The Queen's Token is a historical story
set in Tudor times.

ISBN: 9 780 7136 8850 4 £4.99

Other White Wolves
historical stories...

WAR GAMES

James Riordan

It's Christmas Eve, 1914, and
there's a war on. British and German
soldiers sit in the muddy trenches
either side of No Man's Land, as
deadly enemies. Suddenly, a strange
sound fills the air. A German voice
is singing 'Silent Night'. A British
sergeant joins in, and so begins a
most unusual series of events…

War Games is a historical story set
during World War I.

ISBN: 9 780 7136 8750 7   £4.99

Year 4

Stories About Imagined Worlds

Hugo and the Long Red Arm • Rachel Anderson

Live the Dream • Jenny Oldfield

Swan Boy • Diana Hendry

Stories That Raise Issues

Taking Flight • Julia Green

Finding Fizz • J. Alexander

Nothing But Trouble • Alan MacDonald

Stories From Different Cultures

The Little Puppet Boy • James Riordan

The Story Thief • Andrew Fusek Peters

The Hound of Ulster • Malachy Doyle

Historical Stories

The Queen's Token • Pamela Oldfield

War Games • James Riordan

Outbreak • Alison Prince